THE HAUNTED PLAYGROUND

by Shaun Tan

illustrated by Shaun Tan
Cover illustration by David Palumbo

Librarian Reviewer
Marci Peschke
Librarian, Dallas Independent School District
MA Education Reading Specialist, Stephen F. Austin State University
Learning Resources Endorsement, Texas Women's University

Reading Consultant
Elizabeth Stedem
Educator/Consultant, Colorado Springs, CO
MA in Elementary Education, University of Denver, CO

STONE ARCH BOOKS
Minneapolis   San Diego

First published in the United States in 2008
by Stone Arch Books
151 Good Counsel Drive, P.O. Box 669
Mankato, Minnesota 56002
www.stonearchbooks.com

First published in Australia in 1998 by Lothian Books
(now Hachette Livre Australia Pty Ltd)

Library of Congress Cataloging-in-Publication Data
Tan, Shaun.
    [Playground]
    The Haunted Playground / by Shaun Tan ; illustrated by
Shaun Tan.
      p. cm. — (Shade Books)
    Summary: When Gavin takes his metal detector to a new
playground to hunt for lost objects, he instead discovers a group
of mysterious children who only appear after dark, and who tease
him and try to persuade him to play with them until late into the
night.
    ISBN-13: 978-1-59889-860-6 (library binding)
    ISBN-10: 1-59889-860-4 (library binding)
    ISBN-13: 978-1-59889-916-0 (paperback)
    ISBN-10: 1-59889-916-3 (paperback)
    [1. Playgrounds—Fiction. 2. Ghosts—Fiction. 3. Horror
stories.] I. Title.
PZ7.T16123Hau 2008
[Fic]—dc22   2007003724

Art Director: Heather Kindseth
Graphic Designer: Kay Fraser

Printed in the United States of America

TABLE OF CONTENTS

Chapter 1
The New Playground 4

Chapter 2
Voices 16

Chapter 3
Andrea 20

Chapter 4
The Game 30

Chapter 5
Ghosts? 34

Chapter 6
Time Stands Still 42

Chapter 7
Finders Keepers 50

Chapter 8
Something Worse 56

Chapter 9
When the Lights Go Out 60

Chapter 10
Still the Game 66

Chapter 11
Footprints 70

CHAPTER 1

The New Playground

He couldn't run. It was like being trapped in a nightmare, sinking deeper into a huge puddle of mud with every step. He felt as if someone was catching up to him from behind.

This wasn't a dream. Someone was catching up. Gavin wished that he had never set foot in the park. Now it was too late.

When had everything gone so wrong?

Gavin had discovered the park three days ago. That was late Tuesday afternoon, when long shadows were clues that it was time to go home.

Gavin didn't go home. He had eaten early. At five o'clock on Tuesday he was sitting on a stone wall, watching the crowd of kids scatter. He was waiting for silence and the welcome cover of darkness.

Soon I'll have the park all to myself, he thought, moving his legs so they wouldn't fall asleep.

Gavin would have liked to play with the other kids, even though they were as new to him as the park was. He couldn't. That afternoon, he had more serious business.

His eyes were focused on the pile of steel, wood, rope, and rubber that sat in the beach sand.

It was the biggest playground he had ever seen in his life, and he had seen a lot of them since he got his new metal detector.

Some girls from the nearby school were still hanging around the swings. Gavin kept testing his metal detector against the frame of his mountain bike. He turned the detector's knobs until the machine beeped.

He had first tried out his metal detector on the beach, on a summer morning. He had hoped to discover a lost diamond ring. People were always shaking their beach towels without checking what they had left on them.

After five hours of searching, he had found eight soda cans, twenty-seven bottle tops, and a rusty spoon. He felt cheated.

It was only when he wandered through the beach playground a week later that he struck gold. He found some dollar coins, all underneath a single swing.

From then on his plan was clear. Gavin hunted out every playground within two miles of his house. He drew maps and labeled each site with its own color. He updated the maps monthly.

"It's healthy for a young man to have a hobby," his parents said.

The only problem was the unwanted attention. "C'mon, let us try, let us try!" the other kids would always beg, itching to get their hands on this new, cool toy. They never wanted to stop playing with it.

Even worse, a couple of boys had stolen Gavin's idea and gotten their own metal detectors. Now there were no coins to be found in any of the playgrounds close to home, because everything had been found by those copycats.

So here he was, making trips to new playgrounds at night, when nobody would notice. He was a night searcher, creeping through empty spaces, finding lost property. Finders keepers.

After what seemed like hours, the girls finally got sick of swinging and went home. The coast was clear.

Gavin moved in for the hunt.

He was sure that his work would pay off. Completely sure. In front of him were monkey bars, rope ladders, slides, and swings of all kinds.

Each of them would make bodies jolt and turn upside down. Then loose coins would fall into the soft sand.

This place is perfect, Gavin thought. It's almost as if it was designed just for me!

Two hours later, he was shaking his head in disbelief.

Not because his detector was going crazy and his pockets were popping at the seams with coins. No, because the place was as empty as a sand dune.

He checked all the best places over and over again. Under the corkscrew slides. At the ends of the seesaws. The space around those springy rocking horse things.

Nothing. Not a coin. Not even a flake of aluminum foil. It was very odd.

Gavin tested his detector against the metal bolts around him and it beeped.

Maybe he had been going too fast.

He began waving the detector back and forth, slowly. Still nothing.

It was only when Gavin finally slumped down on a carousel in frustration that he realized how late it was.

Darkness had made the playground into something straight out of Gavin's book on creepy Gothic churches.

The playground was like a huge skeleton, polished in places by a million small hands and feet. Its maze creaked as the wind passed through it.

Gavin shivered and wondered how late it was. He checked his watch. It was missing. His wrist was bare. He looked at the sand around his feet, but couldn't see a thing. How could he have lost it?

There was no way he could go home without it. Next to his metal detector, the watch was the best thing he owned.

What was he worrying about? He had his metal detector with him! He retraced his steps, thinking how smart he was.

There was no way that he could lose anything in the sand.

No way!

By the third time he walked around the playground, he was getting upset. The playground seemed to have swallowed his watch. But he couldn't give up. The watch simply had to be there, and he had to find it. That was all there was to it.

Gavin was on his fourth lap when the playground's light snapped on.

Shadows jumped across the sand as everything was flooded with a ghostly silver light.

Gavin crouched down, like a cockroach caught on a kitchen floor.

Once his eyes stopped hurting from the light, he realized that a playground this big must have a spotlight.

Around the distant edge of the park other lights flickered on, one by one, like orange stars.

CHAPTER 2

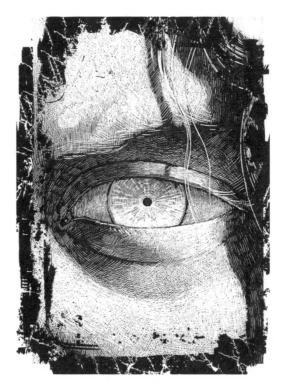

Voices

He was about to get back to his search when he heard voices. They weren't far away, but close. Too close.

Gavin ran to the dark tree where his bike was. He wasn't scared of being seen, but he was shocked at hearing other kids right in the middle of the playground. Where had they come from? Had they been hiding there all along? Watching him?

"Gotcha!" someone yelled. Gavin's heart jumped.

He was about to make a run for it when he heard someone else reply, "Got you back!"

Gavin poked his head out from behind the tree. Five or six boys and girls were climbing through the maze of ladders and platforms, chasing and tagging each other.

Gavin forgot all about his watch and quietly walked his bike away from the playground. It wasn't easy. As soon as he passed the shadow of the tree, the grass felt sticky, like sap, against his shoes.

When he reached the sidewalk, he glanced back. The playground was an eerie pool of light in a black cloud of trees.

Small figures rushed in and out of the equipment. Only one girl stood still, and she was grinning into the blackness, right at him.

Gavin shivered and pedaled back to the lit streets.

CHAPTER 3

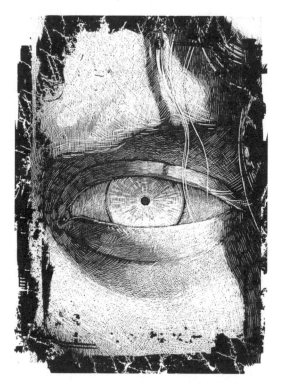

Andrea

Gavin's mother was mad at him for coming home so late that night. "Do you know what time it is?" she asked angrily.

"I lost my watch, Mom," Gavin said.

His father was mad at him for being so careless. "Do you know how much a watch like that costs?" he said.

"I'll go back and look for it tomorrow," Gavin said.

His father grumbled something, and his mother said that next time he should come home when he was supposed to.

The next evening, Gavin carefully walked up to the playground.

He had spent the whole day thinking about the place. He couldn't decide what was weirder, losing his watch or the other kids appearing out of nowhere.

Gavin circled the area twice. After looking everywhere anyone could be hiding, he was certain that it was safe to turn on his metal detector.

He scanned the entire area of sand again for his watch. The detector didn't beep once.

"It's gone for good," he muttered into the darkness. He turned to get on his bike, adding, "You can keep the stupid thing."

As if it was replying, the playground burst into light. "You can have it back," someone said, "but you'll have to catch us first!"

Gavin spun around and saw a girl's back as she ran into the shadows.

The girl reappeared at the top of the tall slide. Her face and hair were pearly white under the electric buzz of the light. She grinned down at him and pulled something out of her pocket.

"Here it is," she said, giggling. She dangled his watch from the tips of her fingers, arm stretched over the slide's railing.

Gavin was shocked.

"Hey!" was all he could shout as the girl let the watch fall into the darkness.

He ran forward, but a small white hand reached out from the shadows and grabbed the watch before it hit the ground.

Then a boy ran out into the light, waving the prize before tossing it to another boy, who was hanging upside down from a set of monkey bars. That boy threw it to someone else. All of them were shouting, "Keep away! Keep away!"

"Where did you all come from?" Gavin asked.

A girl with short black hair jumped down right in front of him, dangling the watch in his face.

"Give it back!" Gavin yelled. He tried to grab the watch. He was sure that his hand had closed around it, but his fist was empty. The girl squealed with delight as she ran away.

Now Gavin was more angry than curious.

He dropped his detector and started to chase the kids.

He ran as his watch flew around. Laughter surrounded him as quick fingers snatched the watch from the air.

They're too fast, he thought.

The watch always seemed to be right in front of him, pulling him into the light. Gavin found himself climbing ladders, balancing on rope bridges, and riding down slides.

Soon he was so tired that he bent over in the middle of the playground, directly under the light. He felt strangely excited by the game.

Once he caught his breath, he noticed that the kids were no longer playing their game.

Instead they were perched like birds, not moving, on the bars around him. They whispered to each other without turning their gaze from where he stood.

"Come on. Give it back, please?" Gavin begged.

"Oh, all right," said the girl he had first seen. She threw the watch down to him.

Gavin fumbled and almost dropped it. The others giggled.

"If you want to play with us, you'll have to learn to catch better than that," the girl said. "And stop running around like you're a blind elephant."

"Who says I want to play with you?" Gavin replied.

He looked at the kids carefully.

They looked different from other kids, with their old-fashioned haircuts and clothes. Also, their skin looked very white. Was that because of the light?

"Where did you come from?" he asked.

"My name's Andrea," said the girl who was obviously the ringleader. Gavin wondered if she was ignoring his question or if she just didn't understand.

Andrea continued, "And this is Beth, Charlie, Dale, Edward, and Fay, in alphabetical order." She pointed to each one of the kids.

"I'm Gavin," Gavin said. The kids laughed at his name.

Some nerve, he thought, considering what their names were.

"So, where did you come from?" Gavin asked again. "This place was empty, and then suddenly the light came on and you were all here."

"We play when the light comes on," said Andrea, pointing her finger at the towering light. "Every night. Like the bugs."

Gavin followed her gaze to a swarming mass of tiny moths and flies. They were buzzing around the light in a wild halo.

Andrea put her hands on her hips. "So, are you going to join us? Or maybe you can't handle it."

CHAPTER 4

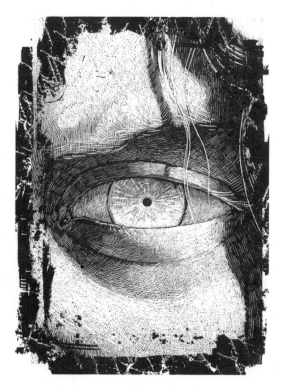

The Game

When Gavin arrived home, it was late, but early enough to avoid getting yelled at by his mom. It had not been easy to leave the playground once he started playing the game with the other kids.

Chasing each other through the playground had been more fun than any other game Gavin had played in his life.

Andrea's crowd of kids was amazing to watch. They had moved in a way Gavin had never seen before.

They were fast and skillful. They knew all the gaps and distances as if they had played the game a million times before.

Gavin knew that when he did get close enough to tag them it was only because they were letting him win.

Even though they made fun of how bad Gavin was at the game, Andrea and the others had not wanted him to go home.

"What a baby," they said. "You should at least stay until the light goes off."

They were still trying to convince him as he wheeled his bike into the darkness. He had to push hard against the grass. It was almost like it had its own gravity.

Andrea had called out, "Well, at least come back tomorrow night, Gavin! We'll always be here!"

CHAPTER 5

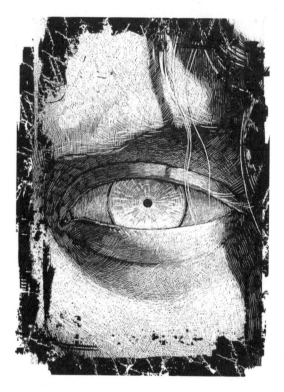

Ghosts?

One of Gavin's friends from baseball went to the old brick school that was not far from the park.

Gavin asked him if he knew Andrea or the other kids. He explained what had happened at the park the previous night.

His friend just gave him a blank look.

"Maybe they're a bunch of ghosts," his friend said through a mouthful of spaghetti and meatballs. "Maybe they haunt the playground because they broke their necks on the monkey bars. Or swings. Or slides. Playgrounds can be really dangerous, you know."

It was just a joke, really. Gavin knew that there were no such things as ghosts, but his friend's comment bothered him.

Gavin decided at that very moment that he would stay away from the park. He had his watch back, and the playground was worthless for detecting metal.

Could the weird children really be ghosts?

It would certainly explain how they seemed to appear out of nowhere, and also their strange appearance.

Plus, some things they said sounded really dorky, like "keen" and "swell."

Only Gavin's grandpa would say stuff like that. The kids had given Gavin a strange look when he once said that something was "awesome."

They seemed real enough when he tagged them and they tagged him back.

It was all too spooky. Besides, he was getting behind in his homework, and his mother was bugging him about being out after dark.

This was all going through Gavin's mind as he stood in front of the playground.

He wasn't sure why he had come, except that he really wanted to.

As soon as the sun set, he started thinking about the games, the laughter, the fun of chasing each other under the buzzing lights, surrounded by a sea of empty darkness.

He couldn't help it. He just had to be there.

Andrea was sitting right next to him when the lights snapped on. She laughed as he jumped back in surprise.

"I shouldn't sneak up on you like that, should I?" she said, giggling. "But I knew you'd come."

"Are you a ghost?" asked Gavin without thinking.

The question had just popped out like a sneeze. Right away, Gavin wished that he hadn't asked it.

Andrea's smile vanished and her face turned a strange shade of green.

"Don't say that word," she whispered.

"What? What word?" Gavin asked, feeling confused. "Ghost?"

"Yes!" Andrea shrieked.

She jumped at him, her thin fingers outstretched.

Gavin screamed as she knocked him to the ground. He waited, expecting some terrible fate, whatever it was that ghosts did to the living. He wished he had stayed at home.

Nothing happened.

When he finally took his arms away from his face, he saw Andrea standing over him with a huge grin.

"Does that feel like a ghost to you?" she asked, bending down to pinch him several times on the face.

The other kids in the playground were roaring with laughter.

Andrea folded her arms.

"Are you going to play with us now, or are we all too scary for you?" she said, smirking at him.

Gavin chased her into the light, feeling like an idiot.

CHAPTER 6

Time Stands Still

For hours, Gavin raced through the playground. He was grabbing poles, scrambling, sliding, swinging, and leaping through the air.

The rest of the world seemed to nearly disappear. Soon, there was nothing but the endless game. It was as if everything else had stopped and they could stay up forever and never have to go home or go to school. It was as if time had stopped.

When Gavin accidentally looked at his watch, he stopped still. It was late. It was very late, and his stomach sank. He realized he'd be as good as dead by the time he got home.

He headed straight for his bike.

"Hey, what's up?" shouted one of the boys. "Don't you want to play with us?"

Gavin sighed. "Yeah, I do, but I have to go home."

Everyone stopped to stare at him.

"My mom is going to be really mad. I'll get grounded for the rest of my life," Gavin said, trying to explain.

The kids looked at him as if he was speaking another language.

"You can't go yet," Andrea begged, running up to him.

"Why not?" Gavin asked.

She paused. "Just stay until the light goes off."

"Don't you ever have to go home?" said Gavin, picking up his bike. "All of you. Don't you have some sort of curfew? Or any rules at all?"

"No! We do what we like," Andrea said, hands on hips. The rest of the group of kids nodded in agreement.

"You're not tired, are you?" Andrea asked.

"No," Gavin said quickly, which wasn't true. "I just have to go."

The group of kids laughed.

Then they were quiet and watched carefully as Andrea pulled a handful of objects out of a bag.

She skipped up to Gavin and opened her palm in front of his face.

There, shining under the light, was a small pile of coins, a silver necklace, and a ring that looked like it had something precious in it.

Andrea said, "This is just some of the stuff that gets lost and left behind. Once something falls in that sand, you can never find it again. Like your watch."

The kids laughed again. Their laughter was more they were making fun of something this time.

Andrea continued, "Wait around long enough and you can collect pounds of this stuff."

Gavin couldn't believe it. He had been hunting for the "stuff" for as long as he could remember and had hardly filled up a single small shoebox.

He was shocked. "How did you get these things?"

Andrea quickly pulled her handful of treasure away from his face.

In a single graceful gesture, she threw it into the night air. It landed somewhere in the playground sand with a soft patter.

"The game begins!" she cried.

Before Gavin knew what was going on, everyone grabbed handfuls of the lost riches from the bag.

As they ran crazily in circles around the playground equipment, the children scattered all of the treasures into the sand.

Hundreds of objects rained around Gavin, ringing as they bounced off metal poles, flashing and spinning.

Once the bag was empty, the kids scrambled up the equipment to perch in high places.

Each of the children was panting with excitement.

The sand was as still and white as the surface of the moon.

Everything had been buried.

CHAPTER 7

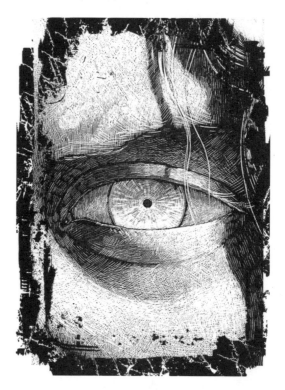

Finders Keepers

Andrea explained the rules as she rocked back and forth on a swing. "It's really simple, Gavin. All you have to do is find as much stuff as you can. Then it's yours. You know, finders keepers."

"What?" Gavin said.

He didn't understand. It was too good to be true. "Come on, what's the catch?" Gavin said.

"There is no catch," Andrea said, smiling. "There is just one rule. You only have until the light goes out. What you don't get now will be gone tomorrow. Back in our safekeeping. The place will be as empty as the night you arrived."

This has to be some kind of trick to make me look stupid again, Gavin thought.

Andrea looked totally serious. The chains of the swing creaked.

"What about all of you?" he asked. "Do we take turns?"

"No," Andrea replied. "We get to watch."

All the kids giggled.

"Now get to work," Andrea told Gavin. "You don't have much time."

Gavin still felt it was some kind of trick.

He switched on his metal detector and used it to scan the ground. It beeped right away. Gavin dug his fingers into the sand and found the first coin.

His audience clapped their hands and talked excitedly to each other.

Gavin barely noticed the noise. All of his attention was on a second coin, then a third, and a fourth.

He soon lost track of how many he had found, as he followed a winding trail through a forest of thin shadows, moving his detector from one sweaty hand to another.

He was hooked. Soon, his pockets were filling up, and no one would even know he was missing at home. No need to check his watch. Not tonight.

He felt free and happy.

He felt as if there was no tomorrow.

He felt stuck in the light.

Sand fell through his fingers and he heard the kids' laughter above him.

As he picked up a thick gold necklace from the space under a tall slide, he wasn't sure if his heart should be beating with so much excitement.

Something was wrong. It was all too easy.

The kids had thrown the treasure around as if it was worthless.

It all looked real, though. Some of the coins were unusual, but Gavin recognized them as the kind of old money his grandpa collected. He knew that the coins were supposed to be worth a lot.

So why were the kids so excited?

Why were they cheering him on while he took their stuff away for keeps?

Would they let him take it away?

CHAPTER 8

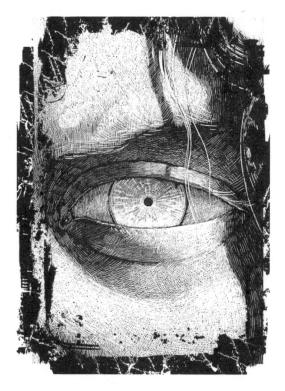

Something Worse

"**Y**ou better hurry!" called Andrea.

She must have noticed that Gavin had stopped.

"The game ends when the light goes out! And you don't even have half of the treasure!" she said.

Gavin smiled. "I can keep going in the dark, you know," he told her.

"The game ends," Andrea repeated.

"I get to keep what I find, right?" he asked.

"We promised," Andrea said, crossing her heart with her hand. "But it won't be much at this rate!"

Gavin looked around.

Something was holding him back.

He wanted to ask a question, but he was afraid the kids would laugh at him.

Finally, he opened his mouth.

"I can go home after the light goes out, right?" he asked quietly.

There, he had finally said it.

Andrea would call him a baby, everyone would laugh, his face would be red as a beet, and that would be that.

Andrea only said one word. "Yes."

The others echoed her. "Yes, yes, of course you can."

Gavin knew instantly that they were all lying.

He realized that all the treasure scattered into the playground was not part of a trick, but something much worse.

It was a trap.

CHAPTER 9

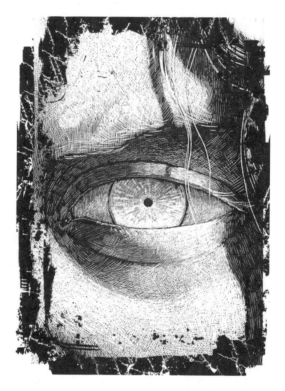

When the Lights Go Out

Gavin watched the kids. They were balancing on high rails, peering through portholes, and hanging upside down like bats. He saw their pale, excited faces in a different way.

They were the ones playing the game. He just happened to be in the middle of it.

A moth flew into the light.

"I have to go," Gavin said. He pushed one more coin into his pocket.

Andrea instantly dropped down in front of him. "You've come this far. You can't just leave," she said.

"Why not?" Gavin asked.

He suddenly felt very nervous. "What do you want from me, anyway?" he asked quietly.

"We just want to you to stay, to play with us. It gets boring, you know," Andrea replied.

She looked past him, into the night. "Always the same place, with the same friends, night after night."

Gavin said, "Just go somewhere new, then. A different playground."

Andrea didn't seem to be listening. "Haven't you ever wanted to play forever, Gavin? To stay up as long as you want, to never have to go home or go to school, or even go to bed? Aren't some games so much fun that they should never have to stop?" she asked him.

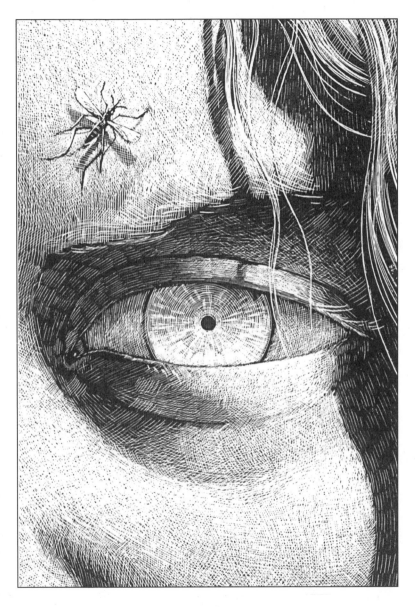

Yes, Gavin wanted to say. Yes, it's so true. He held his tongue, though, as he felt a dozen eyes watching him from between the silvery poles.

"This is what we have chosen," Andrea said.

All of the other children nodded. "And so have you, without even realizing it," she added.

As Gavin backed away, it all started to make sense, in a weird way.

The strange light with which they appeared and vanished.

The way they knew every nut and bolt in the playground as though it was their only world.

They were trapped here.

They were held like insects in the light. They had played too long and too late, and now they could never go home.

Now they wanted him to join them. They wanted him to play until the light went out.

Behind the playground, at the far end of the park, Gavin saw the first orange light flicker and die.

Then the next one.

He dropped his metal detector and ran.

CHAPTER 10

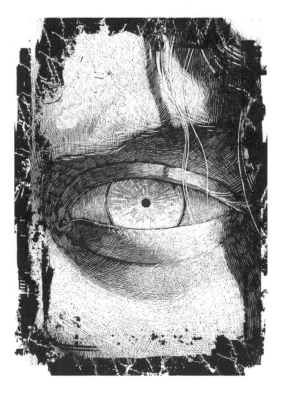

Still the Game

The children chased him, howling with glee. It was still part of the game.

The kids were so quick. They skipped along platforms and bridges as fast as Gavin could run.

A hand reached down and grabbed his shirt. "Let me go!" he screamed, even after he heard his shirt rip. He pulled free.

"No! It's too late now!" one of the children called.

More lights blinked out around the park.

Money fell out of the pocket in Gavin's jeans as he ducked and weaved through the playground, but he didn't care.

He ran across the sand to the edge of the playground and leaped into the grass.

The children were almost on top of him, but he was heading straight for the trees, out of the light, into the safe darkness.

Then his legs began to give up. The ground — no, the light — was taking strength from all of his muscles.

It was like wading through tar. The farther he went, the harder it was to move.

The coins and jewels in his pocket suddenly felt incredibly heavy. They were digging painfully into his hips and pulling him back toward the playground.

Soon he was on his hands and knees, emptying his pockets as more lights went out around the park.

Then the playground light was the only one left. He glanced over his shoulder at the other kids. The light was doing something strange to them, too.

Andrea tried to move across the few feet between them. She looked paler than ever.

"Let me go!" Gavin screamed again.

"Why are you fighting it," Andrea's voice called. "You can play forever!"

Gavin lunged for the shadow of a tree.

A pair of hands grabbed his ankle.

Someone screamed.

The light went out.

A darkness blacker than night swallowed him up.

CHAPTER 11

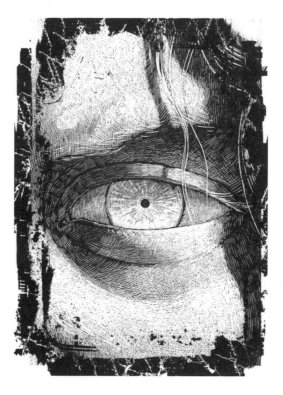

Footprints

When Gavin opened his eyes, the world was a gray blur.

His head hurt really badly. He was covered with dew and the skin around his ankle was badly bruised.

Remembering what had happened, he jumped to his feet.

He was about to run when he realized that he was alone.

The playground was silent and empty in the soft light before dawn. The swings rocked in the gentle breeze.

His metal detector was nowhere to be seen.

All that remained of the night's game was footprints in the sand. They would be erased by the crowds of children who played in the playground during the day.

All the treasure he had spilled onto the grass was gone. The only thing left in Gavin's pockets was a single dirty penny.

I'm dead when I get home, he thought. And I still have to go to school.

Could things be any worse?

He turned the penny over in his fingers for a long time. When he finally threw it back at the playground, it disappeared into the sand without a sound.

ABOUT THE AUTHOR
AND ILLUSTRATOR

Shaun Tan was born in 1974 and grew up in the
northern suburbs of Perth, Western Australia.
In school, he was the shortest kid in every class.
He graduated from the University of Western
Australia in 1995 with a degree in Fine Arts and
English Literature. He currently works full-time
as a freelance artist and author, concentrating
mostly on writing and illustrating picture books.
Shaun began drawing and painting images for
science fiction and horror stories in small-press
magazines as a teenager. Since then he has
received numerous awards for his picture books.
He has recently worked for Blue Sky Studios and
Pixar, providing concept artwork for upcoming
films.

GLOSSARY

carousel (KAR-uh-sel)—a merry-go-round

curfew (KUR-fyoo)—a certain time when a person needs to be at home at night

eerie (EER-ee)—strange and frightening; creepy

lap (LAP)—to travel one time around something. Athletes run laps around a racetrack.

panting (PAN-ting)—breathing quickly and loudly

perched (PURCHD)—sat on the edge of something, often high up

scanned (SKAND)—looked at carefully

smirking (SMUR-king)—smiling in a smug, knowing, or annoying way

DISCUSSION QUESTIONS

1. Gavin met six other kids at the playground. Why were the kids there?

2. What does "finders keepers" mean in this story? What is found in this story? What is kept?

3. Do you believe in ghosts? Why or why not?

4. Explain what happened to the other kids when the light went out at the playground.

WRITING PROMPTS

1. Sometimes it sounds really cool to not have any parents or adults around, like the kids in this story. Make a list of things that would be good about not having adults in your life. Then make a list of what would be bad. Which list seems better? Explain your thoughts.

2. As he plays the kids' game, Gavin finds treasures in the sand. Imagine that you are playing the game, but instead of treasure, you find something frightening. What is it? What would you do next?

3. At the end of this book, Gavin wakes up in the playground and the other kids are nowhere to be found. Write what you think happens next.

TAKE A DEEP
BREATH AND

TRAPPED

BY JAMES MOLONEY

STONE ARCH *Fantasy*

David's new town is boring until he discovers a big drainpipe that looks perfect for skateboarding. He can't resist exploring the huge cement tunnel. Then he hears something odd. Someone else is inside the tunnel, in the darkness, where no living person should be.

STEP INTO
THE SHADE!

Caroline's family inherited a mysterious, old-fashioned doll. Soon after it arrives, Caroline's mother becomes deathly sick. Then the doll starts popping up in some very odd places. Caroline thinks that the doll is out to get her mom. Could a little doll be evil?

INTERNET SITES

Do you want to know more about subjects related to this book? Or are you interested in learning about other topics? Then check out FactHound, a fun, easy way to find Internet sites.

Our investigative staff has already sniffed out great sites for you!

Here's how to use FactHound:

1. Visit *www.facthound.com*

2. Select your grade level.

3. To learn more about subjects related to this book, type in the book's ISBN number: **1598898604**.

4. Click the **Fetch It** button.

FactHound will fetch the best Internet sites for you!